What's Your Symbol?

**by Ms. Beitel's class
with Tony Stead**

capstone

Introduction

Our class learned about symbols. We found out where they came from, what they stand for, and why they are so important. Symbols are important to people around the world.

The Lady of Freedom

by Bailey, Kylee, and Nora

Did you know that the Statue of Liberty is a symbol in the United States of America? It means freedom.

The statue is a gift from France to honor the Declaration of Independence. The French built it and took it apart to send to the United States. They gave it to America to say, "Way to Go!"

If you want to see the statue, you have to go to New York. That is where it is now.

The Maple Leaf

by Beck and Bridget

Hey! Did you know that maple leaves are special to Canada? They are a symbol for Canada. You can find the maple leaf on Canadian money and on the Canadian flag.

The colors of the flag are red and white, and a maple leaf is in the middle. They even have a hockey team called the Maple Leafs. It is a very important symbol in Canada!

The Maple leaf.

Did you know that maple syrup comes from maple trees?

The Palace of Power and Grace

by Chase and Ryleigh

Buckingham Palace is in England. It was built a long time ago in 1703, but now it is a symbol that stands for British royalty.

Buckingham Palace has many guards in fancy red uniforms.

Fact:
Do you want to know why the guards watch over the palace? Because it is the home of the royal family.

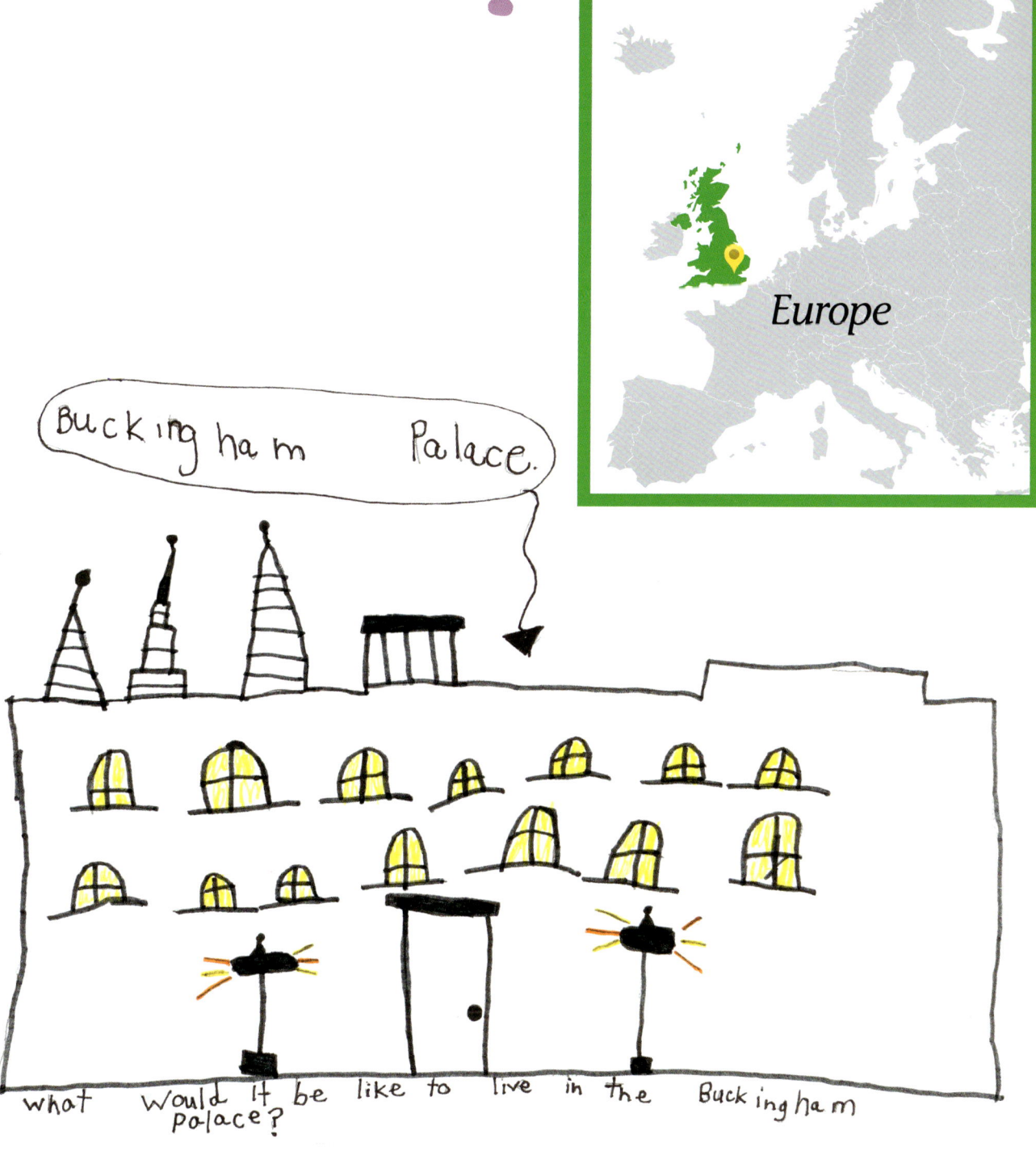

The Iron Lady

by Evan and Liam

France has a symbol, too! It is called the Eiffel Tower. Sometimes the French call it the Iron Lady.

A man named Gustav Eiffel and a team helped build it in 1889. It weighs about 10,000 tons. It's a really popular place to visit.

> **Fact:**
> Many visitors climb the 704 steps every year. How did they count all those steps?

India's Tiger

by Avi, Cole, and Joselynn

Did you know that the Royal Bengal tiger is actually the national animal of India? It is a symbol that stands for grace and power.

Tigers are very powerful! They have sharp claws and can leave scratch marks on trees! If you go into the jungle, you might not see them. Be aware! They are sneaky and dangerous and fast! ROAR!

We had fun learning about symbols. We learned about the Statue of Liberty, Buckingham Palace, the Eiffel Tower, and the tiger in India. ROAR! What is your favorite symbol? Would you like to travel somewhere to see it?